THE JOURNEY OF ALLIS, THE TRACTOR

LEILA WHITE

To order additional copies of this book, contact:
Xlibris
1-888-795-4274
www.Xlibris.com
Orders@Xlibris.com

ISBN: Softcover   978-1-7960-5602-0
        Hardcover   978-1-7960-5603-7
        EBook   978-1-7960-5601-3

Print information available on the last page

Rev. date: 08/28/2019

Acknowledgments

I wish to thank my husband, Frank for insisting we keep Allis in the family. He did everything possible in his power to maintain and protect her.

Thanks to all who encouraged me to finish Allis' story of a lifestyle that is disappearing in our country.

A special thanks to our daughter, Liana. She offered encouragement, ideas and organizational skills to the project.

Dedication

This book is dedicated to my parents Ellis and Gladys Tipping.

Thanks for all the great memories

Hi, I'm Allis Chalmers. The first thing I remember was being rolled off the assembly line in a tractor factory in Milwaukee, Wisconsin, in 1950.

Wow, was I something to see! I was bright orange with all-new parts down to my shiny black tires. I was ready for a home. They shipped me to the Bishop's Tractor store in Webster City, Iowa, which is right in the middle of the United States between Chicago and Omaha. It was spring here, and the farmers were ready to plant their crops. Maybe someone needed me.

While I sat there, Farmer T and his wife and their five children—Elton, Leonard, Ervin, Leila, and Charlene—entered the showroom. Here's hoping they pick me. How could they resist? I'm pretty good-looking. I'm more efficient than those horses he had. The old steel-wheeled tractor he had was really tired and worn-out.

Not to brag, but my ride is smoother and safer with my rubber tires. I know Farmer T loved his horses, but I'll be faster. That old black horse, Prince, sometimes talked back to Farmer T and stopped in his tracks and refused to move.

After looking at me, the family pulled back and whispered among themselves. I knew Farmer T needed me. Mrs. T wondered if they could afford me. I heard Farmer T say, "I can't afford not to buy Allis. We have five children to feed. I need to farm more land. Let's take Allis home." Here I go on my big adventure!

BISHOP Farm Equipment Showroom

SPRING

That spring, Farmer T started to teach me what farming was all about. First, Farmer T and I would plow the field (turning the soil over to expose the good black dirt). We would then disk the soil, which is the process of making the soil finer. Finally, I pulled this neat little planter full of corn or beans. The planter dropped these seeds into neat rows, covering them as we went. It wasn't long before we would see long straight rows of young plants popping through the soil. What joy Farmer T and I felt knowing that our efforts were successful.

Our next job was cultivating, which is removing the weeds from between the rows. Farmer T and I could do this, but the weeds or stray plants in the row would have to be removed by hand. I felt so sad just sitting there, watching Farmer T and the kids walk those rows and cut out what did not belong. They looked tired and sweaty. Every so often, you would hear one of the girls scream when they found a big black-and-yellow corn spider.

When this was finished, the family would need to rely on their faith in God, hoping and praying there would be just the right amount of sun and rain for a good fall harvest.

SUMMER

In summer, we needed to cultivate and fertilize. Farmer T and I were busy in the fields one day, trying to finish our work before the rain started. In the summer, the weather was very unpredictable. A high wind or tornado could appear without warning. On this day, Mrs. T and the children were near the farmhouse, which is nestled between two groves of trees on the north and the west. These trees blocked the winter winds but also blocked the view.

Sure enough, black clouds started to roll to the north behind the grove of trees. Farmer T and I could see them since we were in the field. Suddenly, a funnel of twisting black clouds appeared. Farmer T shouted, "Let's get home quick! It's a tornado!"

We got on the gravel road. My throttle was wide open. Farmer T was standing at the wheel, shouting, "IT'S A TORNADO! GET THE COWS IN THE BARN! GET TO THE CELLAR!"

Farmer T drove me safely into the corncrib and saw the tornado cut across the pasture where the cows had been. It headed straight to our neighbors, took the roof off their house, tore out the trees, and destroyed a building. Thankfully, their families escaped with no injuries.

LATE SUMMER

In the backyard of the house was a huge crab apple tree. I remember one year, the grandchildren were home on summer break from school. The tree's spring blossoms had turned to apples and were ready to be picked. Before I came to the farm, the picking was different. The boys had to climb the tree and shake the branches, while the girls held the blanket to catch the precious fruit as it fell. Now Farmer T and I could take the older grandkids one at a time, lift them up in my front loader, and let them pick the apples.

You've got to love those grandkids, always making my work fun. One day, Farmer T and I needed to pick up the cow poo in the pasture. Cows would leave their poo in neat little piles called cow pies. It's yucky, but it's good fertilizer.

Those cow pies would be thrown into a manure spreader to be spread evenly over the pasture so the grass would grow lush and green. The oldest grandchild, Gregg, drove by at that time and thought, *What a fun job*. Gregg's sister, Liana, heard about the adventure and ran to catch up with me and Gregg. After seeing his sister running toward me, Gregg put me into high gear. Manure was flying high in the sky, spreading evenly over the pasture and also over me and his sister. Mrs. T and their mom, Leila, could see the scene from the house. When we returned, I could see them trying to hide a grin as they told us to stay outdoors and clean up.

FALL

In the fall, it is time to harvest the crops before the snow fell. One fall, the neighbor was working in his field and was hurt very badly, so badly that he could not continue with his harvest. Within minutes, all his neighbors knew of the accident because of the contraption on the farmhouse wall. I later learned this was a telephone with a party line. If you had an emergency, there was a special ring to get everyone's attention. All the neighbors, including Farmer T and I and all my cousins, came to help. Some of my cousins are green (John Deere), red (Farmall), and another orange one like me. Did we ever work together! We saved his harvest. What a cool feeling! We even got our picture on the front page of the local paper, the *Freeman Journal*.

Oh, the fall. It was so great to be part of the harvest. There were big machines for harvesting all the crops. I need to tell you of my favorite harvest story. In the summer, the wheat fields look like a green wavy ocean, but in the fall, the wheat turns golden. First, Farmer T and I would cut the wheat with the mower. Then I would pull this special rake that would scrape up the wheat and lay it in long rows. The binder came next. Farmer T would drive me along the rows of wheat, picking up the wheat. It would disappear into the binder. Like magic, the bundles of wheat were tied up and thrown out the side chute of the binder.

The bundles of wheat were collected by Farmer T's three boys then stacked into piles to dry. These stacks were called shocks and actually looked like giant mushrooms. In my imagination, I could see little gnomes playing in those shocks.

Another job well done!

WINTER

In the winter, the fun started, at least for the kids and grandkids. On Sunday, after church and a big family dinner, I waited in anticipation. Sure enough, here they came with skis and sleds. Farmer T would attach a rope to my hitch. Starting with the younger ones—Shaun, Kent, and Donna—I would pull them on a sled around the snow-covered barnyard. When the yips and giggles died out, usually because the cold had gotten to them, the older kids wanted in on the fun. The ditches along the country roads were filled with snow, making a perfect surface for snow skiing. The kids would grab the rope as I went merrily down the road, watching some stay upright and others tumble into the snow.

After the day's excitement, Farmer T would tuck me into the shed, knowing we'd see each other the next day. He would clean me, grease me, and replace worn-out parts of me, always thinking ahead to the next year.

RETIREMENT

Years later, Farmer T was getting old, and all the kids had left the farm. The decision was made to quit farming and move to the city. I remember sitting there in the barnyard at the big sale. Everything was for sale. I felt so sad. People walked by me, looking me over. Yes, I had a few dings and scratches, but I still ran. Wait, two people stopped in front of me. I know them. It's Leonard, Farmer T's son, and his son, Kent. Leonard looked at me and pondered for a while. Then I heard those beautiful words: "We can use Allis in our lumberyard." Kent started me up. Off we went, racing at twelve miles per hour to the lumberyard that was forty-eight miles away. Can you imagine how many hours that took us?

After a few years of working in the lumberyard, Leonard retired and I was up for sale again. A man with a sawmill bought me. What a sad time in my life. My wheels were removed. I sat there on a platform and rusted away while I cut wood. Then one day, I heard my owner pick up the phone and call to Colorado. I held my breath. That was where Leila, Farmer T's daughter, and her husband, Frank, lived. My owner said, "Frank, do you want Allis?"

I heard Frank say, "Sure do. We'll be right there as soon as we rent a trailer."

It was midwinter, snowing and freezing, as we drove that seven hundred miles to Colorado. It was pretty chilly on that open trailer, but I was open for something new.

Sure enough, something new did happen. Within weeks, I went back to school! Boulder Technology was a school that repaired and restored old cars and trucks but never had accepted tractors. They accepted me. Two students sanded and painted me. Frank replaced my worn-out parts. I think he had sympathy for me since Frank also had so many replacement parts.

Now that I'm restored, I find excitement all over the place. The antique-tractor show at Westminster Mall was my first big hit. Oodles of tractors of different colors were lined up in the indoor mall. Parents placed their children on my seat and watched them pretend to be farmers. There was so much fun for all.

Right in our neighborhood was this old green John Deere tractor. Well, Johnny and I became good buddies. I encouraged him to go back to the same school that I had attended. He came out looking grand. We drove together to the local drive-in for the Friday evening antique show. People ate their hamburgers and drank their shakes while admiring the old cars and us.

Then just when I thought things had slowed down, Frank and Leila sold their home after forty-three years. I was worried as to what was going to happen to me. Lo and behold, they put me on a flatbed, double-decker trailer. Frank backed me onto the top level. All the neighbors stood watching, wondering if he would be able to accomplish the feat. We made it!

We started off on a one-thousand mile, three-day trip to Texas. When we arrived, I thought, *I know these people*. It's Liana, their daughter, and her husband, Keith. Shaking, Keith drove me off my high perch on the trailer. That was when I noticed pastures with mini-Hereford cows grazing. Boogie and Aggie, the cutting horses, galloped by the barn. Chickens were clucking away in their coops. Dogs barked, and cats purred. There was a barn to keep me dry and safe. What more could I ask?

Let me tell you what I have discovered about my new home in Texas. The Baptist church in this little town of Magnolia has a festival called the Pumpkin Patch. They ordered thousands of pumpkins and decorate a grassy lot nearby. I was invited because I fitted right in with the orange decorations and other antiques. Children climbed on me and pretended to drive. Families took pictures.

Best yet, the pumpkins were sold to provide funds for youngsters to attend camp. Pretty neat!

Then you should see the Christmas parade in another small town of Waller. My family decorated me in holiday fair. Adults and kids cheered and clapped as Frank and I drove by. Kids rushed to grab the red-and-white candy canes thrown to them by a grandson. Some giggled because Frank and a grandson, John, were dressed like Christmas elves. Pure fun and joy!

I must tell you of our last adventure. It was Memorial Day in the small town of Hempstead. The town had a parade and celebration to honor one of their citizens, a ninety-three-year-old veteran. The family decorated me and a float to honor all who served in the military. One grandson, John, was in his marine uniform, and another grandson, Josh, was in his army uniform. Even a great-grandson, Mike, fitted into his great-great-grandfather's air force uniform. Red, white, and blue flags were flying. Red, white, and blue candies were thrown to children along the route.

I was so proud to be a part of this tribute to our veterans.

ISN'T LIFE GRAND?

I WONDER WHAT WE WILL BE DOING NEXT!

Lightning Source UK Ltd.
Milton Keynes UK
UKHW050337160822
407353UK00002B/94